To my mother Jan, who has always taught me to question the world
around me and constantly challenge myself to make it better —P.C.

For Dimitri, who has traveled far to help sea turtles —D.H.

For Venus So —M.S.

Text copyright © 2016 by Philippe Cousteau and
Deborah Hopkinson.
Illustrations copyright © 2016 by Meilo So.

Library of Congress Cataloging-in-Publication Data:

Cousteau, Philippe, 1980- author.

Follow the moon home / by Philippe Cousteau and Deborah
Hopkinson ; illustrated by Meilo So.

 pages cm

 Summary: "A book about loggerhead sea turtles, and a girl's
attempts to help save their babies from man-made light."—
Provided by publisher.

 Audience: Ages 5–8

 Audience: K to grade 3

 ISBN 978-1-4521-1241-1

1. Loggerhead turtle—Infancy—Juvenile literature. 2. Rare
reptiles—Juvenile literature. 3. Child environmentalists—
Juvenile literature. 4. Nature conservation—Citizen participa-
tion—Juvenile literature. I. Hopkinson, Deborah, author.
II. So, Meilo, illustrator. III. Title.

 QL666.C536C68 2016

 597.92'8—dc23

 2015001678

Manufactured in China.

Design by Jennifer Tolo Pierce
Typeset in Harriet and Paper Cute.

The illustrations in this book were rendered in watercolor,
colored ink, and colored pencils.

10 9 8 7 6 5 4 3 2 1

Chronicle Books LLC
680 Second Street
San Francisco, California 94107

Chronicle Books—we see things differently. Become part
of our community at www.chroniclekids.com.

# FOLLOW THE MOON HOME

A Tale of One Idea, Twenty Kids, and a Hundred Sea Turtles

By **PHILIPPE COUSTEAU** and **DEBORAH HOPKINSON**

Illustrated by **MEILO SO**

chronicle books · san francisco

I always need help finding my way,
especially in a new place.

"Before long you'll feel right at home, Viv."

I WASN'T SO SURE.

CLASS PROJECT: COMMUNITY ACTION
1. Identify: Find a problem to solve (use your eyes, ask questions).
2. Plan: Gather information and Figure out what to do.
3. Take Action: Put your ideas into action.
4. Tell the story: Show how you—and we—can make a difference!
5. Reflect: Think about what you did and what you might do next.
SUMMER SCHOOL OUTDOOR ACTIVITIES

## "WELCOME, VIVIENNE!"

called Mr. J. "You're just in time for the fun—we're looking for a problem to solve."

I got out my pencil and bit my lip.

I rode my bike ALL OVER TOWN looking for a problem.

(Mostly I just got

L O S T.)

On Saturday, I took Samson and Luna for a run
on the beach. (Mostly they pulled me!)
"LET'S MAKE A GIGANTIC HOLE,"
I gasped, plopping down.

My big digger and my little digger
sprang into action.
Suddenly it was
                    raining sand.

"Looks like fun, but be sure to fill in that hole," said a man walking by. "It's nesting season."

I smoothed out the sand and we all went to look. "What do holes have to do with turtles?"

LOGGERHEAD
TURTLE NESTING
AREA
DO NOT DISTURB

"IT'S BECAUSE OF THE **BABIES**,"

said a voice.

I whirled to see a girl from school.

"I'm Clementine," she reminded me. "Baby sea turtles need a clear path to the sea. Holes and sand castles get in their way."

"I didn't know we had sea turtles here." Samson pulled on the leash.

"We do. Oh, and look what happened to THIS BABY," cried Clementine.

"Why were you going the
wrong way, little one?"

Mr. J had told us to use our own eyes, so that night Mom and I went back to the beach.

As darkness fell, we could see bright lights winking on, one by one, along the shore.

"THAT'S IT!" I said. "THE LIGHTS IN THE BEACH HOUSES ARE THE PROBLEM."

"Why is that?" Mom asked.

"When baby turtles hatch, they follow the strongest light they see," I explained. "So if they head *away* from the sea, they get dehydrated and die."

My heart sank as I stared at the houses.
"There are so many. How can we ask *all* these
people to turn off their lights?"

"Most of these houses are vacation rentals,"
Mom said. "That means new people come to
stay every few days."

"We'd have to knock on doors every night!"

Clearly, I needed help to solve *this* problem.
And I knew

JUST HOW TO GET IT.

On Monday morning, Clementine and I raised our hands first. We told the class what we'd learned and observed about loggerhead sea turtles.

"The sea turtle eggs are starting to hatch," I went on. "To save the hatchlings we need the whole class—THE WHOLE TOWN—to help."

And that's how LIGHTS OUT FOR LOGGERHEADS began.

Our classroom became

# THE LOGGERHEAD LAB.

First we gathered lots of information. We read books.
We visited an aquarium and a sea turtle hospital.
We asked someone from the South Carolina Marine
Turtle Conservation Program to speak to our class.

We all brainstormed solutions, choosing the best ideas.

## THEN WE GOT TO WORK.

We made posters and delivered them ALL OVER TOWN.

We wrote FACT SHEETS for all the vacation beach houses.

LIGHTS OUT FOR
LOGGERHEADS!
LET'S KEEP OUR BEACHES
**DARK**
AT NIGHT, TURN OFF OUTSI
LIGHTS & KEEP CURTAINS
CLOSED Tha

Invitation to
the Town Hall

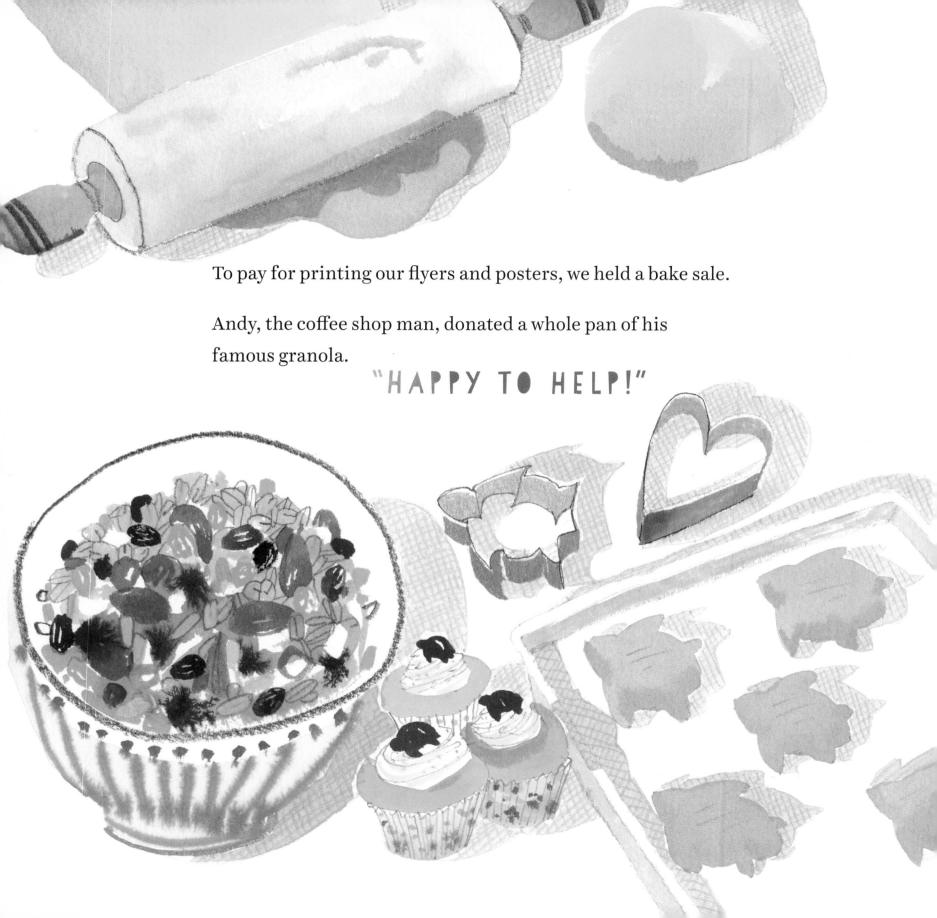

To pay for printing our flyers and posters, we held a bake sale.

Andy, the coffee shop man, donated a whole pan of his famous granola.

"HAPPY TO HELP!"

The editor promised to put my article in the community newspaper. "Nice to have a new writer in town," she said.

STUDENTS LAUNCH LOGGERHEAD EFFORT

Baby Sea Turtles need our help!

The printer gave us a discount. "FOR THE LOGGERHEADS!"

INVOICE 1220
DISCOUNT

Help!
LIGHTS OUT FOR LOGGERHEAD CAMPAIGN
everyone is welcome!

Rebekah and Max learned how to spread the word on the Internet.

Mr. J helped us write a press release. (I was on TV as class spokesperson!)

We invited volunteers from SCUTE (South Carolina United Turtle Enthusiasts) to a town meeting.

When the big night arrived, the room was packed.

The room BUZZED with ideas.

We talked about how to make our beach a great place for turtles:

★ how to MARK NESTS

★ run NIGHTLY PATROLS

★ what to do if hatchlings GET IN TROUBLE

DO KEEP BEACHES DARK: Turn off outside lights during nesting season.

DO STAY CLEAR: Don't disturb nests, adult turtles, or hatchlings.

DO GET INVOLVED: Volunteer! Help protect sea turtles on our beaches!

LIGHTS OUT FOR LOGGERHEADS CAMPAIGN

At the end, we decided to form our own volunteer group.

People cheered for our class.

Mr. J beamed. "I'M PROUD OF YOU ALL."

That was the best night ever.

UNTIL . . .

On the last evening of summer school, we went on a turtle patrol. Lots of parents came, too.

Everyone smiled as we watched the lights along the beach go out, one by one.

We had done it.

Suddenly a movement on the sand caught my eye.

"OVER HERE," I whispered.

We crept closer, careful to stay quiet.

A crescent moon shone on the waves.
The sea glittered like silver.

I made out first one, then two hatchlings.

Soon the sand seemed to boil over
with life.

Tiny turtles,
no more than two inches* long,
burst from the nest.

AWARE !
SEA TURTLE
NEST
Do Not Disturb

*five centimetres

We watched, barely daring to breathe.

WOULD THEY KNOW WHERE TO GO?

# THEN THEY WERE OFF!

Scurrying, scurrying

over the sand

and into the shimmering sea.

We stood together,

smiling and silent with wonder.

Then, just like the turtles, we

FOLLOWED THE MOON HOME.

# LETTER TO YOUNG ACTIVISTS

When I was a little boy I loved to go outside. My grandfather, Jacques Cousteau, was a famous explorer and always challenged me to go out and explore the world. One of my favorite things to do was to visit the beach.

My earliest memory of the beach is from a trip my mother took us on, to Hawaii. Each day we would go down to the beach and explore the tidal pools. We would sit patiently at the edge of these shallow pools of water, not making a sound, and watch as the small fish, crabs, sea anemones, and sometimes even an octopus would go about their business. It was a fascinating world to watch and instilled me with a love of the ocean. Those experiences as a young boy inspired me to explore and protect the oceans as my life's work.

Many years later I found myself walking along a beach in Florida at night filming a TV show about the ocean, and right there before my eyes I was able to watch baby sea turtles—first one, then dozens—crawl out of the sand and down toward the ocean. It is one of the most magical experiences of my life and was one of the inspirations for the story in this book.

If my grandfather taught me anything, it was to be curious, to ask questions, and to dream. Through my work, I get to meet kids every day who are curious, kids around the world who care about the environment and who want to do something to protect it. Like Viv, they realize that they can't leave it up to grown-ups to solve all the problems; they realize that they have to get up and do something themselves to change the world. And you know what? They do. I see kids protecting animals, changing laws, raising money, and more. Kids around the world do amazing things every day, and so can you.

All you have to do is follow Viv's lead and take five simple steps:

First, explore your community, look around, and IDENTIFY something you care about. The world just looks different to kids than it does to adults. That's why ideas and solutions that come from you are so powerful, because you see the world differently and often find solutions where adults don't think to look.

Then develop a PLAN to fix whatever problem you've identified. Research it a little bit—think about the people, places, and animals that are impacted by it and who might want to help you do something about it. Maybe there are conservation groups in your area, or a politician who cares about the environment, or a friend of the family who can help.

Next, TAKE ACTION. There are several ways to do this—maybe organize a community clean-up or do some research with the help of a teacher or mentor that adds to data politicians use to make better laws. Maybe you can raise money through a bake sale or get people to sign a petition.

Then THINK BACK about what happened because of your work. Keep a notebook about who you talked to and what kinds of actions you took. What lessons did you learn? What mistakes did you make, and how did you fix them?

After you have done that, TELL YOUR STORY. Maybe write an article for the school paper, or post a story online—but whatever you do, make sure you tell the world about the great things you achieved so you can inspire other kids to do the same.

And remember, you are not alone. Great resources exist to help. My organization Earth-Echo International is all about helping kids like you to change the world. Visit our website at www .earthecho.org and find out how we can help you.

Every day, young people are changing the world, making it better. I hope you find your special place to explore and to be inspired, just like I did when I was a kid. Then, stand up . . . go out there . . . and change the world, just like Vivienne.

I believe in you.

—Philippe

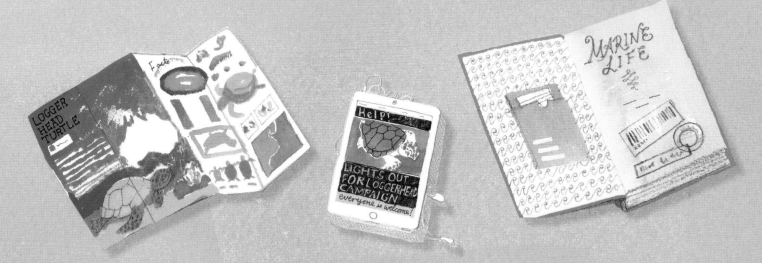

# TO PARENTS AND TEACHERS

From climate change to water scarcity to collapsing ecosystems, the news is dire, and youth are often the first to suffer. The problems we face aren't across the ocean or in some faraway jungle, they are in our communities, outside our back door, in our air, our water . . . everywhere. While that may seem like doom and gloom, *the good news is that the solutions to those problems are all around us, too.*

Every time I see a young person, I see hope. Youth activists have been thought leaders and change makers around huge issues like child labor, civil rights, equal rights to education, and, most recently, issues like environmental justice and immigration reform.

Too often, adults see kids only as volunteers for environmental projects, as participants, rather than seeing them as critical thinkers capable of solving any number of problems.

What can you do as a parent or teacher? First, believe in your children. Allow them to ask questions, and then help them find the answers. When kids are empowered to consider problems, gather information, and drive their own activism by what truly interests them, they invent solutions that adults would often never consider. And those solutions and the passion that they carry into adulthood *will* save the world.

For more information, visit www.earthecho.org.

*Marco Marchi, iStock by Getty Images*

# FIND OUT MORE ABOUT LOGGERHEADS & OTHER SEA TURTLES

The loggerhead sea turtle (*Caretta caretta*) can be found around the globe in the Atlantic, Pacific, and Indian oceans. Named for its large head, the loggerhead is the most abundant sea turtle in U.S. coastal waters. In the United States, the logger-head nests from North Carolina to Florida, with more than 80 percent of the nests found in just six counties in Florida.

This story takes place in South Carolina, where the loggerhead is the state reptile—thanks to kids! In 1988, fifth graders from Ninety Six Elementary School wrote to State Senator John Drummond asking him to sponsor a bill to make the loggerhead the state reptile. On May 8 that year, in the *Spartanburg Herald-Journal* news-paper, Senator Drummond said, "Every time I go to town or to church, one of these children asks me about the progress on that bill." The bill passed!

Loggerheads all over the world are either threatened or endangered, both in the seas and on beaches. That means that while protecting and safeguarding their nesting sites in the United States is essential, it's not enough. There's more to do!

From May to mid-August, loggerhead turtle mothers come to shore to dig their nests and lay their eggs. Each nest has 120 eggs on average. The eggs then hatch in 55 to 60 days, from July to the end of October. Volunteers often find and mark nests early in the season during dawn patrols; and later "nest sit" during night patrols to be sure the babies hatch safely.

In the sea, the greatest threat to turtles is being captured in fishing gear such as longlines and gill nets. Garbage in the ocean, like plastic bags and balloons, is also a big problem for turtles. On land, loggerhead nests and hatchlings are threatened by beach development and artificial lighting on shore.

When baby sea turtles hatch, they instinctively follow the brightest light. On a dark beach, the moon on the water (or whitecaps on the waves) leads them to the sea. But the bright lights of houses and businesses can cause the hatchlings to turn inland. The life of a baby sea turtle is not easy. They face many predators, but they are doomed before they start if they can't reach the ocean.

## SOME RULES FOR WALKING ON BEACHES WITH NESTING SEA TURTLES:

★ Don't walk on sand dunes.

★ Don't shine flashlights, no matter what color.

★ Don't take pictures, even with a cell phone.

★ Don't disturb adult turtles or nests, or pick up hatchlings, or get close when nests "boil" and hatchlings emerge.

★ Do bring the number of your state or local sea turtle conservation group with you and walk to a quiet place to report any problems.

## GET THE WHOLE SCOOP ON LOGGERHEADS FROM NOAA

The National Oceanic and Atmospheric Administration is a fantastic resource for facts on loggerhead habitat, conservation efforts, threats, and population distribution.

www.nmfs.noaa.gov/pr/species/turtles/loggerhead.htm

## SEA TURTLE CONSERVATION IN SOUTH CAROLINA

This story was inspired by the work being done by volunteers dedicated to helping sea turtles. In South Carolina, volunteers for SCUTE, the South Carolina United Turtle Enthusiasts, a group of volunteers dedicated to sea turtle conservation in Georgetown and Horry counties, monitor nests and help control beachfront lighting that disorients nesting female turtles and hatchlings. SCUTE has worked with towns to pass ordinances to limit beachfront lighting.

www.debordieuscute.org/

## YOU CAN HELP!

You can help sea turtles wherever you live. To find out more, visit the Defenders of Wildlife online: www.defenders.org/sea-turtles/how-you-can-help

## INTERNET RESOURCES & LINKS

Daufuskie Island Conservancy, *Loggerhead Sea Turtles*
www.daufuskieislandconservancy.org/index.php?page=sea-turtles

South Carolina Marine Turtle Conservation Program, *Loggerhead Sea Turtle*
www.dnr.sc.gov/seaturtle/cc.htm

South Carolina Marine Turtle Conservation Program, *Lights Out for Loggerheads*
www.dnr.sc.gov/seaturtle/lights.htm

Duke University Libraries, *Sea Turtles in the Classroom: An Activity Guide Correlated to South Carolina State Education Standards*
dukespace.lib.duke.edu/dspace/handle/10161/301